P9-EFI-824

Small Medium & Large

by
Jane Monroe Donovan

To my husband, Bruce, thank you so much for all of the extra help and support you gave me. I couldn't have finished this book without it!

And to my grandfather, Glenn Dowty, who always had such a gentle way with all living creatures.

Special thanks go to my model, Rachel Chambers. She was wonderful with the animals.

—Jane

Sleeping Bear Press™
315 E. Eisenhower Parkway, Suite 200
Ann Arbor MI 48108
www.sleepingbearpress.com

Sleeping Bear Press is an imprint of Gale, a part of Cengage Learning.

Printed and bound in China.

10 9 8 7 6 5 4 3 2 1

Library of Congress Cataloging-in-Publication Data

Donovan, Jane Monroe.
Small, medium & large / written and illustrated by Jane Monroe Donovan. —1st ed.
p. cm.
Summary: A wordless picture book in which a young girl writes a letter to Santa
and receives some special gifts to help her celebrate the holiday.
ISBN 978-1-58536-447-3
[1. Letters—Fiction. 2. Christmas—Fiction. 3. Santa Claus—Fiction. 4. Stories without words.]
I. Title. II. Title: Small, medium and large.
PZ7.D7238Sm 2010
[E]—dc22 2009042136

Santa Claus
North Pole
U.S.A.

CRAYONS
64
Dear Santa,
How are you? How
are the reindeer?
I hope you can find
our new house. I
don't need any new
toys this year but

Cheeri
Oats

Lucky Bones
FISH FLAKES

Dear Santa,

I just wanted to say THANK YOU!

Thank you for my new best friends.

Happy New Year!

Love, Sammy

P.S. Next Christmas, could you please bring a new bone, some carrots, and a toy mouse?

Dear Santa,
I just wanted to say THANK YOU

From the Author

The three animals depicted in this story are actually beloved members of my own household. I had a lot of fun basing this story on them and worked to capture their different personalities and characteristics.

Maylee is a seal-point Siamese and was born on May 3, 2001. When she was little she had very large ears which made her a rather funny-looking kitten, but eventually she grew into them. Maylee sometimes thinks she is one of the dogs and likes to play fetch. Her favorite place is to lie around the back of our necks like a scarf. Another unusual thing about Maylee is that she enjoys being pushed around in a stroller. She gets inside the stroller and sits there waiting for someone to give her a ride. Siamese cats are very talkative and Maylee is no exception. She walks around the house talking with very loud meows. It can be quite annoying, but I think she gets frustrated with us for not being able to understand her.

Grizzly was born on December 2, 2003. His full name is Redlion's Backwater Grizzly. He is a registered Chesapeake Bay retriever. These dogs were originally bred to retrieve ducks from the icy waters of the Chesapeake Bay so they love water. Grizzly also loves to fish. He will stand still in our pond for hours watching the fish. Eventually, he will leap and dive at one, but so far he has been unsuccessful at catching one. Grizzly also loves to open presents. At holidays we have to put the presents up high so he can't open them. Sometimes we wrap extra presents just for him; he goes wild ripping off the wrapping paper and tearing open the boxes as fast as he can. He's happy if he finds a stuffed animal or bone inside.

Fern is a miniature horse and she was born on May 11, 2005. When people see Fern they usually think that she is a foal and expect her to get bigger. But she won't get any taller. (I think the only thing that seems to get bigger is her belly.) The farm from which we purchased Fern delivered her to us in their minivan. Fern lives in a pasture with two full-size horses named Ameera and Lena. One spring day the horses were feeling their oats and began running all around the pasture, and up and down the hills. Fern was running behind Lena when Lena suddenly stopped. Not being able to stop in time, Fern ended up wedged underneath Lena. They were stuck that way for a few minutes before breaking free. Both horses were fine, though I think a little bit in shock.